I Need You More Than I Love You and I Love You to Bits

I Need You
More Than
I Love You
and I Love
You to Bits

Gunnar Ardelius

TRANSLATED BY Tara Chace

FRONT STREET
Asheville, North Carolina

Originally published under the title
Jag behöver dig mer än jag älskar dig och jag älskar dig så himla mycket
by Rabén & Sjögren, Sweden, 2006. Published by agreement with the Pan Agency.

Copyright © 2006 by Gunnar Ardelius
English translation copyright © 2008 by Tara Chace
All rights reserved
Printed in the United States of America
Designed by Helen Robinson
First U.S. edition, 2008

This edition was produced with the support of the Swedish Arts Council.

LIBRARY OF CONGRESS CATALOGING-IN-PUBLICATION DATA
Ardelius, Gunnar.
[Jag behover dig mer an jag alskar dig och jag alskar dig sa himla mycket. English]
I need you more than I love you and I love you to bits / Gunnar Ardelius ;
translated by Tara Chace. — 1st U.S. ed.
p. cm.
Summary: Morris and Betty, two teens living in Stockholm, Sweden,
meet and fall in love but the darkness within each of them at times
makes it hard to maintain their love affair, especially after Betty compares
Morris's behavior to that of his bipolar father.
ISBN 978-1-59078-472-3 (hardcover : alk. paper)
[1. Love—Fiction. 2. Manic-depressive illness—Fiction.
3. Mental illness—Fiction. 4. Stockholm (Sweden)—Fiction.
5. Sweden—Fiction.] I. Chace, Tara. II. Title.
PZ7.A678Iaan 2008
[Fic]—dc22
2007049004

FRONT STREET
An Imprint of Boyds Mills Press, Inc.
815 Church Street
Honesdale, Pennsylvania 18431

I Need You More Than I Love You and I Love You to Bits

ONE

Her foot slides over and then back, cautiously
stroking the toes of his left foot. His head quivers
when he glances up and catches her gleaming
eyes, as wide as five-kronor coins. He blushes,
noting the soft tug at his heart.

"Where'd you learn to kiss like that?" She tilts her head and looks down at the cuticles.

"Like what?"

"Like how you do."

"I learned it from another girl."

"Ah … Pity. I thought you taught yourself on your hand."

The room is red, everything in the room is red:
the carpet, the bedspread, the wallpaper, a big,
fuzzy teddy bear like you win at the fair. Even
the threshold leading into the room is red.

"Do I dare go in here?" He senses right away
how silly he's being. Then he doesn't manage to
think anything else. She shoves him brusquely
into the room, though with a smile that exudes
something else. Shuts the door so the music and
the hum disappear, and lies down on the bed. He
doesn't lie down but walks around the room a
little aimlessly, picks up a Barbie doll with its hair
dyed red.

"Do you think she dyed the hair herself, or
can you buy them this way?"

"Come here for a minute, lie down instead
and you can play with the dolls later."

Dad is bipolar. That means that he gets a rune
tattooed on his right arm when he goes to
Iceland; that he takes up smoking when he's
forty-seven; that sometimes he leaves an
enormous tip when he eats out; that he laughs
louder than other people and cries more quietly.
But most of the time it doesn't mean anything.

It's going to haunt him, he understands that even
now. The sweet, stuffy smell in the room, her
blotchy face that melts into everything else. She
pulls up his shirt so his stomach shows, then does
the same thing to herself and presses her bare
midriff against his. "Skin," she says, scrunching
her eyes and mouth into the middle of her face.

The first thing he sees when he wakes up is the clothing strewn in black patches across the floor. Wrapped in a blanket, he goes downstairs to the living room. The coffee table is covered with beer cans, and someone has curled up into a little ball in an armchair. Stepping cautiously he goes back up the stairs again. The red room is paler in the morning light. He gently shakes her until she wakes up.

"So, what was your name?"

"Betty."

"I'm Morris. Can we meet again sometime?"

Mom's ceiling has a crystal chandelier. It clashes
with everything else in the apartment: the
children's drawings on the walls; the big piles of
newspapers and notepads that have been scribbled
all over; the floral-patterned sofa and the rice
pillow you sit on. The crystal chandelier is an
heirloom. Now it's lying on the kitchen table
split apart into hundreds of dusty pieces. One by
one she dunks them down into a bucket of water
and soap, then takes them out and gives them
to Morris who dries them with a rag. That's her
method, he thinks, to devote a ton of energy to a
small detail and let what's out of control keep on
being uncontrollable.

The light and the warmth disappear, moving on to somewhere else. It doesn't matter. They sink into the coming darkness. There were some howls coming from a couple of people drinking beer and sitting around a tape recorder. Betty points to one of the people, a guy with a face that in the twilight looks like it consists mostly of nostrils, two big holes.

"I made out with him last week. It was really great, actually."

Ice shoots through him for a second before he gets that she's joking.

"But he was sniffling the whole time, so I was forced to tell him to leave," she says, at the same time leaning into him so she ends up with her cheek against his throat.

"I've been thinking about you," he says after a while. "I was really happy when you called."

"Well, you said I should."

He tries to breathe as normally as possible.
"Yeah, but not that you should call the same day."

The hot dog stroganoff sits pathetically on the table. Dad gives him so much, it overflows the plate. It's always hot dog stroganoff when he comes to visit. "Why do anything else when I'm so good at this?" he says. It's weird to be there when he's cooking. "Here's how you do it," he says, carefully cutting the onion and hot dogs into precise cubes. He uses the half-cup measure for the cream, a tablespoon for the tomato paste, and a quarter teaspoon to determine the proper amount of salt.

"I thought about you all day today. That I was
going to meet you tonight. The expression
you would have when you met me. The way I
would open my mouth when we kissed, sort of
half-open so you would switch in the middle
of the kiss and turn it into a French kiss. How
we would walk down the street, which display
windows we would stop in front of, and which
ones we would just walk by. About all the people
who would see us and wonder what fun place we
were off to."

They open their jackets in the wind and lean out
over the railing, as if they were about to take off
from the Västerbro Bridge and sail over the city.
The air is so clear and cold that their eyes sting.
There's no limit to how far they can see. She
looks at him, how his cheeks have turned red
from the wind. He looks at her, at her hair that
seems like it wants to flutter away from her head.

Her stomach is wet with sweat, her belly button
has turned into a little pool of water; he forms
letters with his index finger.

"What are you doing?"

"Writing."

"What are you writing?"

"*Morris was here.*"

The sheets make a muffled, rustling noise
when she sits up. What he wrote disappears into
the folds of her stomach.

She pours milk into the coffee. In his head he
counts the number of seconds she lets it flow. He
gets to five seconds before she sets the milk down
and drops in two sugar cubes. He makes a mental
note of that: five seconds, two cubes. She drinks
the coffee in a slightly different way, submerges
her upper lip and slurps up a few drops at a time.
Her actions sink down into him like stones in
wet cement. They've known each other for a
week and four days now.

"If anything interesting happens, I just think how
I'll tell you about it as exactly as possible later.
Today on the way to school I saw an earthworm
that had dried onto the asphalt and was stuck
there. If I'd told anyone at school that, they
would've just laughed. But when I thought about
the earthworm, I was totally sure you would
understand. It was just hard to wait all day."

"What did you think?"

"That it looked sad."

A scrap of paper tumbles out of his jacket pocket,
crumpled and old. She picks it up off the ground,
trying to read a few words. They're written in
pencil, blurry, and jotted down carelessly. When
he sees the scrap, his face freezes up and he holds
his hand out for it.

With both arms he pulls the comforter over their heads, fluffs it up so it forms a little tent.

"Time has stopped in here," he says, huddling against her. "Under this comforter our names are Peanut and Sailor, there aren't any other people, and we're going to live here forever, maybe have some little brats who think this bed is the whole universe."

"How will we get food?"

"There's no need for food. We'll live on hugs and kisses. And if we want something after all, then we can just order out for Thai food."

"I'm starting to find it a little hard to breathe," she says, gasping for air. "Would a little breathing hole be all right?"

She wakes up because she laughed in her sleep. It's light and sunny out. It's shining on his face, which looks a little younger when he's asleep, more open and more relaxed. His mouth is pressed against the pillow, where there's a little puddle of drool. Shaped like a little heart, she thinks. Under the covers it's warm and smells like their bodies. She rubs against him until he wakes up.

"We can eat breakfast in my room if you'd rather."

She's leaning against the door wearing a T-shirt and underwear.

"I'm coming. I just have to get dressed." He sniffs at the doorway. Smelling the scent of coffee and toast. When they trot down the stairs he sticks close behind her.

"Ah, the young master and mistress have seen fit to greet the day already?" Betty's mom says, walking over to them and smiling. She hugs Betty and then, to his surprise, hugs him, too.

"Here's your seat, Morris. I boiled your eggs for seven minutes."

She pinches a piece out of the slice of bread and
rolls it into a little ball, takes another piece of
bread and rolls it up the same way. When she's
rolled up twenty bread balls, she starts dunking
them in strawberry preserves, one by one so they
resemble small gooey berries. The crusts are still
lying on the table, looking pathetic. "You can
have them," she says. "I don't like the crusts."
When she's done dunking the balls, she puts
them in a bowl and fills it with milk until they
aren't visible anymore. Then she takes a spoonful
of sugar and sprinkles it over the milk.

Dad's wearing his reading glasses and is leaning over the Saturday crossword puzzle in *Dagens Nyheter*.

"Come help me out, Morrie. I have to finish this before we can go to the game."

"But the game starts in half an hour."

"Yeah, that's why I need your help so much."

He's filled in almost all the boxes in very meticulous handwriting. The writing doesn't go outside the lines anywhere; rather, it stays inside. It seems like a really depressing crossword puzzle: *alone* intersects *naïve*, which intersects *mislead*.

"There's just this word left now, a nine-letter word for *pigment products*."

"*Paintings*," Morris says. "It has to be *paintings*."

"Well, I'll be damned. I think that's right."

Dad slaps him on the back and a warmth spreads through the room.

The team scores a goal and Dad abruptly moves
closer, his hands fumbling hesitantly; he pulls
Morris to him and gives him a peck on the cheek,
a little wet and stubbly. After the game they go to
Pelikan and drink an aperitif of Bäska Droppar,
then eat egg-and-anchovy salad on dark rye and
drink beer. Dad laughs so loud that a man in the
group next to them turns around and stares.

"Do you think crazy people are drawn to each other?"

"Yeah, I think the ones who are insane choose each other to be able to put up with it at all. Then the ones who are left can be drawn to each other to their hearts' content."

"But if the crazy people get together with other crazy people, then the children should be total fruitcakes. And their children in turn would be walking vegetables."

"The sickest ones probably don't have any kids; they kill themselves instead."

Mom talks about her dreams, reads poems she's
written, and tells stories about Sixten's adventures
in the Congo. He's a guard at an airport. One
day he saw someone throwing empty bottles over
the barbed-wire fence to another guy standing
on the outside who stuffed them into a suitcase.
Sixten went over and asked them what the heck
they thought they were doing. The man threw
himself down at Sixten's feet, crying and begging
not to be fired. "Okay, I'll let it go this time,"
Sixten said.

The rag rug at Mom's house is still on the floor of
the hallway. He lifts it up and peers at the floor
underneath; it has a different patina there—
untrodden. He remembers the rug as rainbow-
colored, that he used to let his fingers run along
the edges of the different fabrics, naming the
colors to himself, names that only he knew. Now
the colors in the rug have all been washed out
and turned gray.

"Come here, I have to check something." She
stretches out her arms toward him. "I'm going to
count all your moles and write the results in my
blue book. I'll count them every day from now
on. Surely we can agree on that?"

He stole a postcard from Mom. A soldier's black
silhouette stands out against a large sun, and
the Swedish flag is planted the same way the
United States flag is on the moon. It says *Posted
for peace* at the top. It's from Sixten. He turns
the postcard over. "Thinking about you a lot,
missing you more," he wrote.

"Sometimes when you look into my eyes I have to look away because it feels like you can see what I'm thinking."

"Well, I can. Right now you're thinking about my stomach, here where there's a little roll of fat."

"No, I'm thinking that you're a chemist and that I'm your molecules, Morris molecules. You're trying to make a potion out of me, a love potion that you will give to people who don't have any love in their lives."

"Now you're thinking that my hand is cool and feels nice against your throat."

It swings back and forth in him. The thought
that they'll stay together, then that they won't;
both are frightening. Her hard collar bone and
the softness that slopes below it. He can choose
between the alternatives.

"My taste has changed. The love songs on the
radio have started describing how everything
really is. I'm not sure I can deal with being
happy, it feels like I'm made out of play dough.
I don't want to be in love like that, like all the
other boring people. Our love is different. It's
about us."

"I want to know everything you've ever done."

"You're not going to think it's that interesting."

"Why did time even exist before we met each other? To me it doesn't feel like it did."

"For me there's a before. It's like a boundary, everything good on one side and everything bad on the other."

What if everyone in the world were the same—

except two people. He looks at himself and then
at Betty. Her hands disappear into a big white
cloud of soapsuds as she does the dishes, but
they're still in there, submerged, he can be sure
of that. She holds out her wrinkly hands and
sets them in his lap and lets him wipe them dry
with the dishtowel, and the skin on her fingertips
slowly stretches back out. When her skin acts that
way he wants to say to her, *We belong together like
Hennes & Mauritz. Those people out there aren't us.
Don't go.*

TWO

She sits down on his knee in the crowd, flicks her
lighter, and holds the flame down toward the
grating. "Do you see? There's an old bus pass,
one of those big ones with a picture on it. I
wonder how long it's been lying there."

"Shouldn't we put something in there, so
that our grandchildren can come here and be
amazed?"

"No, just a secret sign for the two of us, no
grandchildren." She digs around in her jacket
pockets with both hands and pulls out a
coin. "We'll throw this fifty-öre coin in; that
symbolizes eternal love and happiness. We'll kiss
it so a little of each of us sticks to it."

Wasn't it true that he'd understood as early as that
first morning when she opened her eyes that they
would stay together? He can't tell anymore; the
way he remembers her changes all the time. In
the future the way he feels now will be distorted.

"That's what scares me, how sometimes when

I talk to you it starts bubbling out of me. I say things I thought would be private."

"Like what?"

"The thing about the cavity in my tooth, for example. I tell other people that I've never had a cavity, because I don't feel like that teensy one counts. But when you ask, I have to tell it exactly like it is and then I notice that I've almost forgotten the truth. Because I've said something else so many times."

"Well, isn't that good, then?"

"I mean, you could ask about anything. I'm not sure I'll tell the truth about everything."

There's a pendulum on the desk in Dad's office.
It has five silver balls that move back and forth
in an unfaltering arc. On the desk there are also
big piles of job applications. Morris slices open
an envelope with a letter opener made of black
wood.

"'Hi, my name is Gunnar,'" he reads aloud
from the application. "'Since the age of three I
have …'"

"Toss the letter," Dad says. "You can't have a
name like that here."

He sits alone in the office for a while and waits
for Dad's meeting to be over. The pendulum
ticks back and forth. When Dad comes back he's
got a couple of crumpled grocery-store bags into
which he starts scooping the applications.

"These are the unlucky ones, and we don't
want people who are unlucky."

He looks out over Lake Brunnsviken. At the glass
walls and ceiling of the SAS building, at the
highway embankment's attempt to keep out
the grime and noise, at the Scandic Hotel, and
at Statoil's unintelligible logo. Then he turns
his head and looks at the Museum of Natural
History and the Wenner-Gren Center. Betty
is somewhere behind all of this, behind all the
unimaginative buildings and asphalt gray roads
built by middle-aged men. For a moment a mild
sense of panic grips him. What would he do if
she didn't exist? Go to museums, live in a hotel,
build highways?

"Before I met you I could try on a pair of jeans
and think: What does it matter if they're a perfect
fit? The funnest thing I'm going to do today is
still going to be getting to watch a rerun of
Beverly Hills 90210. I might as well buy a black
plastic bag. That would be cheaper."

"I take it you never did walk around in a
plastic bag."

"No, I usually bought boring clothes that
would match my boring life. Or I bought
fun clothes and hoped they would change my
personality. The ugliest thing I ever bought was
a fluorescent pink vest. Somehow I got it into
my head in the fitting room that it looked good.
After that I had a sense of dread for more than a
year every time I opened my closet until I gave it
away to a charity."

"Tell the one about when you punched in the code
and you felt like you were melting." He burrows
his head into her armpit with his nose as far in
as it will go. This is how she smells, exactly like
this.

"Yeah, I felt so in love, like a melted snowball.
And when I went to punch in the code at the
front door of your building, I thought about all
the times your fingers pressed those numbers
there and how those fingers were so lovely in
me."

"And then you stopped outside my door and
wondered what you would say when I opened
the door."

"Yeah, even though I never said it." She turns
so they can look into each other's eyes.

"What were you planning to say?"

"I was planning to say that I was a little
nervous."

"Here's the gay beach. In the evenings they gather here." They're strolling around Lake Brunnsviken and he's telling her about the various places they pass, even though they've walked there lots of times. Betty isn't from Stockholm, after all, so it can't hurt for her to hear a repeat of the lesson in local geography, history, and folklore. She's wearing a charcoal gray denim dress, which they both helped to pull up. Her black tights sag around one of her ankles. He holds the white underwear tightly in his left hand.

"Do you think you'd want to be with me if you
    could read my thoughts?"

        "Everything you were thinking?"

        "Yeah."

        "I'm not sure. How would I know that?"

        "You can't."

They lie hidden on a flat rock on the north shore
of Lake Brunnsviken. He looks at her feet
submerged in the yellowish water. Her toes look
like little cheese curls.

"I used to come here in middle school to
sneak cigarettes." He takes off his socks and
dunks his feet in the water so they end up
next to hers. "First I took off all my clothes so
they wouldn't smell, smoked a cigarette in my
underwear, and then went for a swim afterward."

"Exactly what we're doing now, in other
words."

"Yeah, like now, only lonelier."

"You have to promise you won't laugh when you
see it."

"I promise."

"You can't think that I look like a monster."

"Just show me."

He pulls up his shirt and on the side of his
stomach is a birthmark with a hair growing out
of it.

"Is that all?"

"Do you think I'm disgusting?"

"It's hardly even visible."

"Sixten came home and we got engaged." Mom's voice is eager on the phone, it sounds like a frenzy of flying spit on the other end.

"We went to a spa this weekend, ate sushi, took mud baths, walked around all weekend in bathrobes, everything was included, although not the champagne, we had to pay extra for that, and we had our own room to sleep in, the room was all designed to look Japanese. Totally amazing. Everything was great."

The phone goes silent for a while.

"Well, how fun. I guess congratulations are in order, then. Congratulations!"

"Yes, and now he's gone off to his regiment."

"I added a different spice today, can you guess
which one?" Mom scarfs down the food
enthusiastically to show that she thinks she made
something really exciting. Sixten turns his head
toward Morris and makes an effort to look like
he's also curious what the answer is.

Morris looks down at the plate; the vegetables
are covered with brown dots. "Is it cinnamon?"
he asks uncertainly.

"Cinnamon on vegetables?" Sixten mutters
and then goes back to eating.

"Good guess!" Mom's whole face beams,
feeling understood. "I thought it would go, and
for dessert I made crème caramel."

cold | membrane | open | journey | why | coffee
costs | think | sidewalk

Mom got a little transparent box of refrigerator poetry magnets. "I've decided to have a new poem on the fridge every day." It's too much work when she talks about stuff like this; her eyes get sort of cross-eyed, and then he realizes that she is completely serious. He positions himself behind her and massages her shoulders with his thumbs. She is soft and hard at the same time. "Not so hard," she says, wincing, "it's nicer when it's a little softer."

The highlighters are available in various bright
colors: pink, green, and orange. He doesn't know
what color Betty wants, but he guesses yellow.
Her books are filled with these kinds of yellow
lines, so you can tell what's important. The sales
clerk stands in a corner of the shop; it's a young
man wearing a black T-shirt with white lettering:
Kafka didn't have that much fun either.

"Excuse me, do you have yellow
highlighters?"

"Fluorescent markers?" The man's dry facial
skin tightens in an expression of self-importance.

"Yeah, maybe that's what they're called."

"No, we're out."

"You don't have any in stock?"

"No, we're out. You'll have to choose
something else."

He goes over to where the nonfiction books are,
and when no one's watching he tears pages out of a
book on wine tasting until his fingernails hurt.

"Tonight we're going to listen just to this." She
skips ahead to "Mute Witness" and hits repeat.
"What we do tonight will be stored in this song.
Every time I put it on from now on I'll feel
exactly like now. So if you die, I can still have
you."

"If I die?"

"Or if you are paralyzed and can't lie in my
bed all night anymore."

"Lying there would be exactly what I could
do."

"Yeah, and then we can listen to this song
together."

"Have you told your dad about us?"

"He calls you the *Bettster.* Aren't you taking the Bettster to the party? Aren't you taking the Bettster to this or that?"

"Couldn't I meet him?"

"I don't know."

"I'd really like to."

"We'll have to see. He works a lot."

"My bike broke. When he found out, he took
the whole day off from work and I got to stay
home from school. Then we went out to Solna
Centrum mall. 'You have to be able to ride your
bike,' he said. After the bike shop, we went to the
liquor store. 'I'm going to buy wine for my wife,
I'm tired of being frugal,' he said and bought six
expensive bottles of wine. I got that something
was wrong with him, but everything was so fun
and exciting, so I didn't want to ask what."

The down that's all fluffy right where the cheek
turns into the throat. It's almost like it falls off
when he touches it; *peach fuzz*, she calls it. He
takes one of her fingers, her index finger, and
looks at the nail. The half-scraped-off red nail
polish. With his front teeth he nibbles off small
flakes that don't taste like anything, it's just nice
to putz around a little.

"Have you been up in the Eiffel Tower?" he
asks, drooling out little red bits.

"Yes, but you already knew that. So why are
you asking?"

"What a view, huh? France, as far as the eye
can see."

"Are you making fun of me?"

"Now you're in for it." He rolls over on top
of her, looks her seriously in the eye until her
breathing changes.

The darkness comes, the way it usually comes.

The light is sucked out, leaving a vacuum. He blinks and feels the warmth like a kind of cold. Knows that he doesn't have to do anything besides wait. Sometimes you have to wait only a little while and sometimes you have to wait a long time.

The covers bulge in the grainy night air. She's
lying underneath, that he can be sure of. He
crawls up from the foot of the bed, slips down
next to her, and stuffs one of her breasts into his
mouth as if she were breastfeeding him in her
sleep. He listens to the sounds, the city noises
outside. Apart from that there's no noise.

Sometimes she asks what he's thinking about.

Once he responded that he was thinking about them breaking up, that he was wondering if they really were made for each other. He wanted to be on his own. Actually he was thinking about something completely different, something about how he could write a formula for solving the Rubik's Cube. She cried all day and he enjoyed her inconsolability, how she wedged herself in, pounding on him with her fists and saying that he could never say that again.

They go for a walk in Betty's neighborhood. A
ribbon of asphalt stretches out ahead of them,
meandering along between small soccer fields,
playgrounds, and fruit trees.

"I could get used to this," he says contentedly.
"The calmness and the considerate people."

They walk by a man standing with his back
bent and his face leaning over a pile of steaming
dog poop. One of his hands is covered by a black
bag.

"It frightens me that I can't do anything sensible about it."

"Are you scared that you'll wind up with a boring job where you have to see the same people every day and drink instant coffee?"

"I'm more scared that I'll forget the feelings I have now."

"Kind of like how you forgot how it feels to be three years old."

"That surely I'll wind up thinking: I was so young, I didn't really understand everything. It bothers me that I know I will be wrong."

She presses a button and the whole village comes
to life. A model train starts chugging along, and
the windows of the little houses light up. Each
house has a yard with a bright green lawn. Her
dad built a little miniature civilization up in the
attic.

"He doesn't like me being here."

"Don't you think it's great?" He looks out at
the big table, everything seems so peaceful and
controlled.

"He shuts himself in here for hours."

"Does your mom like being in here, too?"

"No, she hates it."

"Why are we always at my house?" She stretches out her arms to show that this is precisely where they are.

"Everything is so cozy here in your room, I feel more at home here than at my own house. I can hardly remember the color of the sheets in my room."

"White, maybe? Surely we could be there sometime when they're home? One time at your mom's place and one time at your dad's?"

"Um, in that case there's something I have to tell you. My parents aren't really like yours."

"Well, there wouldn't be any point in visiting them if they were, would there? It would be weird if they were actually exact duplicates of my parents and that you've been hiding them so I wouldn't die of shock."

"My mom's place is a little messy. She doesn't care that much that it looks like that. She mostly writes poems and goes to various study groups."

"I think that sounds like an ideal mother."

"And my dad is even weirder in a way that's harder to explain."

"Is he mean?"

"Not mean, but it's a little hard to relax when he's around. He can get really intense."

"Well, like how?"

"Like, if we go to a soccer game, for example, then he always kind of jogs the last part of the way there because he gets so excited by the crowd and wants to get to the stadium as soon as possible."

"But," she breathes the way she does when she's thinking about something, softly but spasmodically, "then he acts just like you."

Everything in front of his eyes goes cloudy and starts spinning. He must have a weird look in his eyes, because Betty looks totally frightened. He gathers up his stuff off the floor and shoves it halfheartedly into his backpack. He'll get the rest some other time. Right now he just has to get out.

When he stops and looks around he notices that he has no idea where he is. It's starting to get dark, lots of people are passing him on their way home from work; their feet scrape against the gravel in the asphalt and their breath is showing. He goes into a flower shop. It's humid and smells almost perfumed. "I'm not buying anything," he says. "I just have to warm up a little somewhere while I think." A balding old man with a comb-over is standing behind the counter. He sets down a blue flower in front of him and cuts a bit off the stem.

"In the beginning, being alone is always a choice.
Then it's not a choice anymore. When did it stop being a choice? What is it in me that stopped choosing you, that moved into you instead so that I have to be with you in order to be with myself?"

"You have to get the sadness out so it can go
away."

"But what am I going to do? When I get
to a certain point, it runs out, it just turns into
silence."

"You have to find your way in. That's the
hard part. You use up so much energy staying
closed off."

"I suppose I'm scared it will never end if I
open up."

They get out of the car in the gigantic parking lot.
The asphalt is hot and smells like summer. The air hangs, quivering over the ground. Morris watches Betty as she tries to peel off her sticky sweatshirt; after a minute her head peeks out, red from the effort.

"There aren't that many people who chose to make a major shopping run today," Dad says. "But cool that you guys wanted to come along." Then he starts walking with determined steps toward a building filled with a long chain of shopping carts.

"I'm sure most people are at the beach on a day like this," Betty says, pulling out a cart after inserting her coin to release one.

It's cool and peaceful in the store. They walk in a line, all three of them, each with a shopping cart. The refrigerated displays make a dull rumbling noise. Dad goes first and cheerfully mumbles his way through everything on the shopping list, first to himself and then out loud. There's a shelf with various jars of preserved fruit. Dad takes down a big jar of pineapple and holds it up in front of him.

"This goes well with ice cream. A bit of an everyday extravagance."

"I escape into you and you escape into me. But we can't just trade places. I want you to still be in there when I enter you, otherwise I'll drown."

"We're together anyway. Ultimately it doesn't matter where."

"There should be something between people, a table where you put a part of yourself and discuss it from the outside."

"I don't need a table like that."

"How will I know who I am, then?"

"Do you remember what you were wearing when we met for the first time?"

"Was it my red-and-black-striped shirt?"

"Yeah, it was. Do you remember the pants?"

"My black cords?"

"Yeah, and you had your nice underwear on because you wanted to wear nice underwear the night you met the love of your life."

"I don't remember that."

"Is that what I am, the love of your life?"

"I've only ever been in love with you and with a girl in nursery school named Saba. You win over her."

"Did you crochet this just for my sake?" He holds

up the potholder and sees her face through the
loops. "When did you have time to do this?"

"In my spare time."

Something breaks inside him, an ice dam; he
can't hold it back when he sees the asymmetrical
rag with his initials in elegant blue letters.

The snow comes in heavy, wet flakes. No one can see them lying there at the top of the diving tower in northern Djurgården. The tops of the pine trees across from them are drooping under the weight of the wet snow. He had decided to bring her here a long time ago, before they'd even met. There's no helping the fact that it's winter. The whiteness slowly covers the blanket over them. Being together is being far enough away from everything else.

THREE

"Have you noticed that I've been a little different
today?"

"In what way?"

"That I've been acting weird in certain
situations."

"Nope, I haven't noticed that."

He has a picture of Betty from the first morning.

"Are you one of those perverts who photographs everyone you sleep with," she had asked. "Yup, that's just what I am," he had responded. The picture is grainy and black-and-white and mostly just of her face, a face in full morning sun. It should be the picture of her that gets grainier every time he takes it out, but that's not how it works. It's something inside him that's getting grainy.

"How can I know that you really like me?"

With both hands he's holding her around the neck in a stranglehold.

"Because I say so."

"Because you say so?"

With a jerk she pulls herself free from his hold. "Do you have to be so skeptical? I'm sure you get what I'm saying."

"Yeah, I get what you're saying. That's not what worries me. It's how you're saying it."

She sits in the bay window with her back to the
window and smokes a cigarette with her left
hand, her other hand is inside her underwear.
From the red leather sofa he can see the contours
of the knuckles inside the white cotton like small
tapered hills. She takes a puff, turns to face the
window, and tosses the butt through the narrow
opening. Walks barefoot over the herringbone
parquet to him on the sofa and puts the palm of
her right hand over his face, pulls the hand over
his face until her fingers reach his mouth and
pushes them in. Her fingernails scratch the flesh
on the inside of his cheek, and an acidy bitterness
spreads through his mouth.

Will the skin around her chest and throat develop

spots now? He feels her birthmark on her inner
thigh, a meatball tadpole where the friction
makes his hand linger. There's something he has
to say. How do you say something like that?

Her whole face is in simultaneous motion, it's like looking down into a pot of boiling stew. Her body moves rhythmically, interpreting intentions in the course of events and reacting to them. It's not like that for him. There's nothing to work against. He closes his eyes and feels the swell of her breast with his fingertips. There is a blemish on the skin. He has to feel it and feel it.

He's naked, his body is used. Betty smiles at him
as if he's done something good, caresses his hip.
How will they go on? What will they do now?
He's going to put his clothes on again. He's
appalling like this.

"That's what happens to us when we die, threads
go in all directions all the time. I just want you
to understand that." He turns over to face Betty
in the darkness and sees her chest moving up and
down. He leans over her face and holds her hair
out of the way with his hands so he can see her
whole face. Everything is so rhythmic, so balanced
when she's asleep. They can talk about everything
together when she's like this, but not when she's
awake. Now is when he opens up for real.

In the dream she has a big red beach ball that
she's rolling in front of her in the snowy white
sand. She smiles at him, the kind of smile that
makes him feel like something is melting inside,
like something is softening. Her swimsuit is also
red, red with black polka dots, which makes her
look like a ladybug. She's running toward him
but never seems to really get there. Every time
she gets close it's as if the scene starts over again
from the beginning. He tries to walk toward her,
meet her partway, but the sand does something
to his feet, makes him sink down a little bit with
every step. So he just stands still and watches her
coming toward him until she disappears again.

Dad's eyes sparkle like two solar eclipses, solid
black hiding the light behind them. The light
glimmers a little around the edges. He runs his
hand through his hair so that the dandruff snows
down like silver glitter over the collar of his shirt
and his shoulders.

"Dad." He happens to enunciate the word as if
he really wanted to say something important but
has no idea how to proceed. Something ulcerous
grows in his mouth.

"Why didn't you turn in the coupons like you
said you were going to?"

"I forgot. Sorry."

He has an image of his dad standing up at Ale's
Stones, Sweden's Stonehenge. The image
consists of the grass, the sea, the sky, and Dad.
It's like three layers, three equally large lines
lying on top of each other: the grass on the
bottom, then the sea, then the sky. Dad is
standing exactly at the precipice between the
grass and the sea with outstretched wings. That's
what it looks like. He can see a series of images
before him, how first Dad cheerfully waves
good-bye a few meters up in the air, then an
image when he opens his pill holder, a red plastic
one with different compartments, one for each
day. In the last image white pills are falling like
snow onto the grass.

"He wasn't exactly sulking, but you know what I mean."

"Was he irritated?"

"Not exactly irritated. He was sort of like that time you were going to come and meet him."

"Was he irritated then?"

"It doesn't matter; at any rate it was a little tiresome."

"It matters to me."

"Okay, I guess he was a little sullen."

"Why couldn't you just say that right away?"

"I thought you understood that from the beginning."

"That he wasn't exactly sulking but sullen?"

"Well, it's not like I can read your mind."

"It's easier if you actually want to know what I'm thinking."

"It feels like you went and made up your own
mind about who I am, that I won't change, just
because that's easiest for you. It seems like you
don't want me to act differently." She tries to
make eye contact, but he looks away. He just
doesn't have it in him to look her in the eye
when she's saying the kinds of things he knows
deep down inside are true. It's too hard. He
doesn't say anything and she keeps going. "I've
noticed that I've started to act the way you
think I should. I don't intend to be that kind of
person. Before it felt like you thought I could do
anything and then I believed it, too."

The bus is about to pull away from the stop. The
door by the driver's seat is closed. He jogs along
with the bus as it starts moving, tries to look in
and make eye contact, but the driver ignores
him.

"Can't you open the door?" he yells, panting
and knocking on the door. "Open the fucking
door!"

The driver stares straight ahead and drives
away.

He runs and runs, sees all possible colors
swimming before his eyes, doesn't manage to
catch the bus at the first stop, but keeps running,
he can't stop now or he would vanish. He finally
catches it, watches dejectedly as his ticket gets
stamped, walks to the very back of the bus, and
there he can't hold it in any longer. The tears
come like ribbons.

Will she call soon? His arms and legs curl away
from him like syrup; the way he stands in the
room when no one sees him, with his back
hunched and his arms hanging limply. He raises
his left arm and sticks his nose in his armpit.
What do people do when they're lonely? He
doesn't know.

He writes down a word to remember it. Later on when she comes, he goes and gets the scrap of paper and holds it up in front of her. For a while it's all there at the same time: in his head, on the scrap of paper, and in front of him.

He has a picture of himself dressed up like a Native American. His mom took the picture; she took almost all of the pictures. If anyone came up with the idea to collect their family photos, then the pictures of her would be worth the most. The sense of pride at the big feather headdress washes over him again; which is to say, it hadn't left him, that feeling, but had just been dormant, waiting for him to become a chief again.

The postcard was postmarked in Paris on April 9,
1978. It's from their honeymoon. On the back
it says *Greetings from PARadISe.* It's written in
Mom's handwriting, with a small heart over the *i*
instead of a dot.

"I don't think every person is unique. If every person is unique, then *unique* is a completely unnecessary word."

"Don't you think that every person has something specific that makes them special?"

"Maybe, but if that's the case, then people are 99 percent boring."

"And you, are you one of the few people who isn't boring?"

"I don't think I'm any more remarkable than anyone else. The difference is that I've discovered that I don't need to go around pretending I have a personality."

"I drank out of a mug today."

"How exciting."

He keeps going without paying any attention to her contribution.

"There was a little map of the Parisian subway system on the mug. There were tons of lines in different colors that were spread all over the city. If you want to travel between two stations, there are several ways you can go. Not like here in Stockholm. When I go to see you, I always have to change trains at the main T-Centralen station."

He picks up her T-shirt from the bed and buries

his face in it. The feeling of safety spreads around him like warm bathwater. Imagine living the rest of his life without this scent that only she has. He can walk into a room and sense that she was just there, perceive the pungent sweetness she leaves behind.

"Why are we so boring all the time? Can't we do something fun?"

"Sure, like what?"

"I don't really know, anything as long as it's fun."

"Maybe we could rent a movie."

"That might be nice."

He stands up, walks out into the hallway, carelessly throws on his coat, and yells good-bye without waiting for a response. It's dark out. A parked car with its lights left on casts an eerie light over the street. He walks for a ways until he passes a grove of trees, where he stops for a brief moment and then walks in among the trees. He sits down on a big rock, a boulder. Feels deserted in an exciting way. As if he's capable of being alone.

She's lying in a puddle on the bathroom floor,
wrapped in a black silk robe with a dragon
embroidered on it in gold. Her toes and fingers
are all curled up. He wants to say that he's sorry,
too, that he dies when he sees her like this.
Instead he turns off the bathroom light and lies
down next to her, becomes a part of their ball of
yarn.

Snores that slice through the darkness wake him
up, as if someone is trying to start a lawn mower
over and over again. A thought comes over him,
a salvation.

"Wake up, Betty, wake up." He shakes her
eagerly. "You have to wake up."

"What is it?" She turns toward him, but her
eyes are still closed.

"Well, I was thinking that we could take a
trip, maybe to Paris. Try new foods, snails or
frog legs, go to museums, do some wine tasting,
anything you want."

The car glides silently along local roads after the freeway ends in Norrtälje and the speed limit drops to thirty miles per hour. It smells like leather, he thinks, or new-car smell. Outside the trees and plants are waiting for spring to arrive so they can start to grow unchecked. Big piles of gravel lie by the sides of the road, and the leaf buds have a light green sheen. Betty's dad is holding the steering wheel with his arms straight and looking straight ahead. She's sitting up there next to him in the passenger's seat and glances back at him in the backseat now and then. She says a few encouraging words. "Won't it be great?" or "We stop here a lot to buy coconut balls."

They're lying on their stomachs in front of the
wood stove, which shoots out sparks every now
and then. An orange square glows surrounded by
black. He moves his hand toward it and shuts his
eyes, feeling the heat against his palm.

"Are we here because we're having a crisis?"
she says in the middle of exhaling.

A shower of sparks erupts as if the stove were
choking on something.

"I don't know," he says hesitantly. "I've never
had a relationship before."

"It feels like we're being pursued."

"What do you mean?"

"As if we have to go out all the time and go
for walks, because if we're not going for a walk
then something terrible will happen, something
will catch up to us."

Two birds with strange curved beaks are standing
down by the edge of the beach and tugging at
something that seems to be stuck in the sand.

"If only we could stay here forever." There's a
note of sadness in her voice.

"Here in Singö?"

"Everything would be so easy then.
We would prepare meals, go for walks, go
swimming, and go to bed early. Maybe buy a
good dessert on the weekends. We could just be
with each other."

"Yeah, but that wouldn't work. We wouldn't
be able to take it. One of us would go crazy after
a couple of weeks, like that guy in *The Shining*,
and try to cut the other one up with an ax."

"I don't get it. We're doing everything right,
aren't we? It's all the other people who are always
getting in the way. I want to get away from
them."

"But that's just Morris and Betty. We're Peanut
and Sailor. We're sitting on a boat on its way to
America along with Kristina from Duvemåla—
you know, from the musical—and all her nice
friends. When we get there we'll buy cotton
candy and root beer and watch TV shows in our
house in North Carolina. It's a fantastic little
house with a view of a river where redfish jump
up and down. In the backyard we have a pool
where the water is so blue that you think the sun
went and lay down for a while. I'll be a stay-at-
home mom and buy an apron decorated with
little pockets filled with candy. Our neighbors'
names are Brandon, Kelly, Dylan, and Steve."

Their breath shows when they exhale. They're
standing on the balcony with vegetables wrapped
in aluminum foil in their hands. As if they were
thinking about handing out Christmas presents.

"We could actually make them in the oven,"
he says, shivering.

"We said we were going to barbecue," she
replies, determined, setting down the vegetables,
which gleam in the darkness on the balcony
floor. Then she bends down under the grill
and takes out the lighter fluid, sprays it over
the briquettes until the container is completely
empty. It forms a pool under the briquettes,
which aren't able to soak up all the liquid. With
her left hand she runs a match over the striking
surface, back and forth a couple of times until it
ignites. Then she flips it into the barbecue.

It's lying there, squashed into the ground, with
a horseshoe-shaped wound. If it weren't for
the quills, it would be hard to tell what kind of
animal it was.

"Horseshoes don't seem to bring good luck to
hedgehogs," he says to cheer things up a little.

She flips the animal over with two sticks
and makes noises like a detective who is piecing
together what happened. The tips of the sticks
turn red. "There are some things that not even
a hedgehog can protect itself from," she says
tactfully and then starts walking again, hopping
over the carcass.

"How do you know when it's over?"

"Maybe when you feel more in love with your memories than with the person standing in front of you."

For a while it feels exactly like before, like she

can joke around any way she wants, fool around
however she feels like without thinking about
it. Just be silly to the point that everything feels
warm and jolly. A grass skirt is hanging on the
wall; just the fact that there's a grass skirt hanging
on the wall makes them both laugh. She pulls it
down from the wall, slips it over her head and
shimmies it down over her body until it comes
to rest above her hips. She puts on a show until
every bit of grass in the skirt is vibrating. Then
takes off what she was wearing underneath and
runs out in the yard with him right behind
her. She screams, feeling happy. She wants to
scream all the blackness out of her body. When
she stands and sticks her hands under his T-shirt
and feels all the smoothness that is him, she feels
tingly. She wants to lie down there on the green
spring lawn and just listen to the rustling from
the grass skirt while his hands touch her.

She's standing out on the balcony looking out over
the gray-green water. Then she lowers her eyes
and looks down at the pier where he's lying and
waiting with his legs dangling over the edge.
He's already dragged the rowboat out of the
water and tied it up to the pier again. She catches
a glimpse of two bright-red life jackets in the
boat. They had planned to row over to the other
side and buy salmon at the fish farm. It starts in
her stomach. It always starts in her stomach, a
growing, black clump of tar. She tries to think
positive thoughts: The salmon will be great to
barbecue. Maybe they can take a dip by the
rocks and rinse away all this ice-cold water. It's
just impossible to be happy about all the pleasant
little amusements they try to think up. There's
something fundamental that's missing, something
she can't put her finger on. It's like they're always
pouring more multicolored sprinkles on top of
melting ice cream.

They're sitting on the red leather sofa and crying
all the tears that they've stored up recently. It
feels frantic, everything they say disappears into
sobbing and runny-nosed, incomprehensible
words. Every time he looks at her he just wants
to throw himself into her lap and say that it was
just a joke. That they're still together, that they're
still going to do thousands and thousands of fun
things together. It's impossible to understand how
two people who love each other so much can
hurt each other so much. "Why can't everything
just be the way it usually is?" she cries. "I don't
know," he answers. "It just can't anymore." He
tries to lift his arm to take a drink of water, but
his arm won't obey. He sinks down off the sofa,
down onto the herringbone parquet flooring,
and she sinks down after him as well, so that
they both end up on the floor. "Couldn't I have
a hug?" he asks. *Yes, sure you can have one*, she
thinks, *but just one. Otherwise I'm going to go crazy.*

They hug as hard as they can, desperately hard. It
feels like every hug they've ever given each other
at the same time. Their mouths glide toward each
other, they haven't truly understood it's over,
no one has thought to tell them the tragic news.
They get closer to each other as if it's the most
natural thing in the world, as if they've always
belonged together. When their lips brush against
each other their bodies give a start and roll apart,
across the floor. They're flung apart like two
repelling magnets. That's what's happened. Their
plus and minus poles aren't attuned to each other.

"You know that night we went swimming by City
Hall?" Her eyes twinkle. She's speaking more
straight out into space than to him specifically, as
if she's remembering something out loud.

"Yeah, what about it?"

"I snuck a peek at you while you were getting
undressed. I thought, 'Morris, he's the only thing
glowing in all this darkness.'"

"But there were probably thousands of lights
on the other side of the water and over by the
subway tracks."

"I know, but I wasn't looking in that
direction."

Inside his body dark red fireballs leave his heart
and gush out, warming his hands and feet until
they singe and burn and forget themselves. His
hands fumble, his body is a transatlantic liner
and smoke billows out of his mouth in the lit-up
darkness. Nameless girls look down at him and
up at him and through him. His skin gets goose
bumps and the small pinpricks from their gazes
bore into the places where they were always
rather painful. His chest fills with wet cement,
he feels a twinge and he doesn't know if he's
bursting or hardening.